THE COMET OF DOOM

The Story of Halley's Comet

ANDREW DONKIN

Illustrated by Gillian Hunt

MACDONALD YOUNG BOOKS

When beggars die, there are no comets seen;
The heavens themselves blaze forth the death of princes.

From the play 'Julius Caesar' by William Shakespeare,
who saw Halley's Comet in 1607.

Prologue

Woodlands in Kent
4.39am, 21 April 1066

An animal howl pierced the night, waking
the boy with a jolt.

He waited until his eyes adjusted to the
pitch black around him. Then, moving slowly
and silently, he crept past where his parents
still lay sleeping and out into the dark.

Outside, the night-time forest was a blanket of rustling animal sounds and the chill of the pre-dawn dark made him shiver. The boy looked up towards the sky, but the new spring leaves on the trees blocked his view.

Although he knew he shouldn't wander far, the boy headed up the slope towards the top of the hill. The ground under his feet was wet and muddy.

He suddenly froze as a noise rustled towards him through the thick forest. An adult deer, antlers held high, sprang out of the blackness and raced away.

The boy breathed again and continued his climb through the woods.

Finally, he stepped out of the trees. Stretched out before him was the night sky. He could see as far as the horizon in all directions.

Hanging there, silent in the perfect blackness of space, was the comet – a glittering silver firework with its tail spreading across a quarter of the sky.

This was what the whole village was whispering about. No one knew why it had appeared, but everyone agreed that it was a bad omen.

He had heard
many things about the comet:
that it was an angry star, an evil
spirit, and even that it was a sky beast
– a fiery monster that lived beyond the
world. The boy gazed up at the beautiful
silver visitor and somehow found it hard to
look away.

Chapter 1

A street market, London
6.30pm, 5 September 1682

"Buy a lucky charm, Sir?" shouted the
woman, holding out what looked like a small
coin. "Keep away the evil influence of the
comet," she added, pointing upwards
towards the twilight sky.

Edmund Halley looked up to where the great comet loomed in the sky over London. The market trader did not know that she was talking to a scientist who had spent his whole life studying the sky and the stars.

Halley reached into his pocket and handed over a penny piece.

"Tell yer friends," she shouted after him, happily. "Keep 'em safe too."

Halley walked through the market. All over town, people were going about their business with a sense of unease and worry. It seemed that everyone feared the comet.

Something caught Halley's eye and he paused to take a closer look.

"It's a comet egg, sir," boasted the trader. "Saw it laid this morning with my own eyes."

On the shell of the egg was a marking in the shape of a comet. Halley licked his thumb and ran it over the marking. It smudged.

"Doesn't mean it ain't real," snapped the man, indignantly snatching back the egg.

Halley left the market and headed towards the north side of Piccadilly. He held his nose as he stepped over the foul-smelling liquid running along the gutters.

Waiting inside the Piccadilly Coffee House was Halley's friend, Isaac Newton.

Newton was one of the greatest scientists of all time. He had discovered gravity, the nature of light, and more recently, this new coffee bar.

"I hope you have some good gossip for me," said Newton, as Halley sat down.

"Gossip? All anyone will talk about these days is what new disaster the comet will bring. And how it will be the end for us all," sighed Halley.

"People will not stop being afraid of comets until science can explain what they are," said Newton, "and predict when they will appear."

Both scientists knew that the planets in

the solar system - Mercury, Venus, the Earth, Mars, Jupiter, and Saturn - travelled around the Sun in circular paths called orbits.

The movements of the Sun and all the
planets were neat and ordered. But comets
were quite another matter.

"They come and go exactly as they please,
with no rhyme or reason," said Halley, as if
their behaviour were a personal insult.

15

"Perhaps this will help," said Newton handing over a stained and scruffy notepad. "If you're ever going to complete your work on comets, you'll need as many different observations of them as possible."

Halley opened the notebook. Inside he found page after page of observations of the great comet of 1531. Observations like these from the last century were like gold dust.

They were just what Halley needed to add
to his own studies of the current comet.

By the time the two scientists finished
their discussion and headed home it
was late in the evening. The
streets sparkled like silver,
lit from above by
the comet.

Chapter 2

Edmund Halley's home
11.38pm, 19 September 1682

Edmund Halley was watching the heavens
move. His telescope viewer was centred on
the comet as he followed its slow progress
across the night sky.

Every night for the last fortnight Halley
had taken careful note of the comet's
exact position, its brightness,
and the length and
direction of
its tail.

He noticed
that, for some reason,
its tail always seemed to point
away from the sun.

Observing the comet was hard work
because Halley knew that to calculate its
orbit would require very exact measurements.
He leaned back in his chair and rubbed his
tired eyes.

"Can I have another look?" asked a voice.

"Help yourself," said Halley, with a smile.

Taking care not to move the telescope, Rob looked through the eye piece. Rob was ten years old and liked to think of himself as Halley's assistant. He sneaked a look through the telescope whenever he got the chance.

"I was telling my dad what you said about the comet being no danger and that," said the boy.

"What did he say?" asked Halley.

"He just gave me a thick ear and told me to get supper ready."

Halley adjusted the telescope, as he had a dozen times already that night, making sure that the comet was central in the viewer. Without needing to be asked, Rob handed him a pencil and the astronomical chart.

The boy watched the scientist make a note of the comet's new position.

The words were a mystery to Rob. Like most children, he could not read or write, but lately he had begun to pick up bits and pieces from Halley and he was always keen to learn more.

"We'll find out the answer to the comet problem however long it takes," said Halley.

Rob shifted uneasily and looked down at the ground. Halley knew him well enough to realise when something was wrong.

"What's the matter?"

The words exploded out of Rob.

"I might have to go to the countryside because dad says that the comet will bring another plague and he doesn't want to be in the city when it comes and he's going to make me go with him and I want to stay and help you," said Rob, without pausing for breath.

"There's not going to be a plague," said Halley, looking straight into Rob's eyes. "Comets aren't evil things like your father believes. They obey the same laws as the planets and everything else in the solar system."

"No plague?"

"No plague."

Halley leant forward again to make the next adjustment to the telescope.

When he looked up, Rob was ready to hand him his pencil and the chart.

Chapter 3

Edmund Halley's Oxford home
4.21pm, April 2 1696

As he walked through the busy Oxford street,
Rob held the package as if his life depended
on it. Inside was a new lens for Halley's latest
and most powerful telescope yet. Now in his
twenties, looking after Halley's telescopes was
a full time job for Rob.

He crossed the street dodging between
two riders on horseback. He clutched the
new lens close into his chest to keep it safe.

Halley's house was just around the next
corner. Rob quickened his pace, anxious to
get the heavy glass lens inside.

"In here!" bellowed a voice as soon as he had stepped through the door.

"I've done it. I've finished the calculations," continued Halley, as Rob entered the study. As always the room looked like it had been hit by a hurricane.

There were star charts all over the floor, and on the tables. Tall stacks of books threatened to fall down if you even looked at them.

In the middle of it all sat the scientist, pen in hand, scribbling notes. Always scribbling notes.

For the last six months, Halley had locked himself away from the world and had thought about nothing but the comet problem.

28

"I have calculated the orbits for twenty-four comets and I am finally sure that one of them *does* keep returning."

Halley stood up and, with Rob's help, spread out some large charts on the floor.

"Look at this. This is the 1531 comet's orbit, and this," said Halley pointing to another chart, "is the 1607 comet's orbit."

Rob looked from one chart to the other. Both orbits were exactly the same shape.

1531

1682

1607

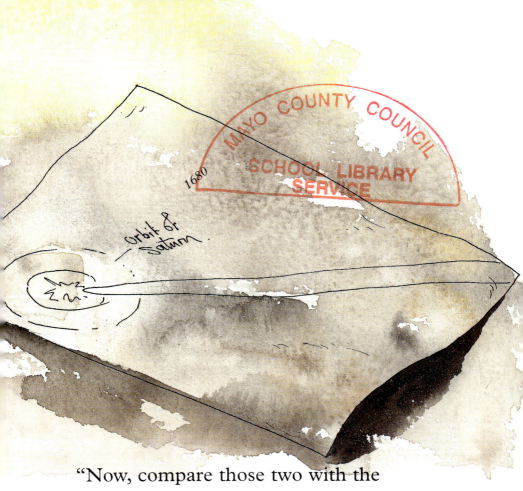

"Now, compare those two with the 1682 comet we saw together," said Halley pointing to yet another chart.

"It's another orbit the same shape," said Rob. "But what about this one?" he asked.

Halley looked. "*This* chart shows the orbit of the 1680 comet. The orbit is so long, it stretches right off the page," he laughed.

"But the orbits of the 1531, 1607 and 1682 comets are so similar... I'm sure that they show the same comet coming back century after century," said Halley, slumping back in a chair.

"We must tell everyone at once," said Rob, with great excitement.

"No one will believe me now," said Halley. "The only proof that I'm right will be when the comet comes back again."

"When will that be?"

"It returns roughly every 76 years.
That means the next appearance should
be December 1758." Halley looked sad.

"I won't be alive to see it, but you might
have a chance. Rob, you've got to promise
me something."

"Anything."

Halley leaned forward. Rob had never
seen him look more serious.

"Don't let them forget my prediction.
Make sure someone looks for it. Make sure
they remember," whispered Halley.

Chapter 4

A country farm, near Dresden
Christmas Night 1758

Johann Palitzsch stepped out of the warmth
of his farmhouse and into the freezing
winter's night.

The Christmas goose had been eaten, the
presents unwrapped, and now the whole
family was asleep, all except for Johann.

Johann was a farmer by profession, and an astronomer whenever he got the chance.

It was a clear night and the stars looked bright and sharp. He set up his telescope on the same wooden barrel as always and trained it towards the sky.

Getting ready for Christmas had kept him busy and it had been more than a week since his last search. He felt like he was looking for an old friend. He focused the telescope and scanned across the familiar pattern of stars. Then he caught his breath.

Something was different.

In the centre of the pattern was an extra star. The new star was blue, slightly blurred, and behind it was the beginnings of a tail.

There was no mistake. Johann had found it. The comet was returning – just as Halley had said it would.

Whooping with delight, Johann ran back into the farmhouse and woke everyone up to tell them. For the Palitzsch family, the real Christmas was just beginning.

Tomorrow he would send word of his discovery to England, where a very old man called Rob waited anxiously for news.

Epilogue – The Future

ISS Newton – An international
space station orbiting Earth
2.15pm, 29 July 2061

"… So Halley was proved correct and the
comet has been named after him ever since."
 The crowd listened, fidgeting impatiently.

"But I know what you really want to do is see the comet for yourselves, so let's head for the observation deck," continued the guide.

The ISS Newton had opened for business six years ago – a home for scientists, students and sightseers five hundred miles above the surface of the earth. Now in 2061, the comet's return could be watched from space.

Somewhere in the crowd of people was
Edward.

Edward was not the smartest kid in his
school, or even the most hard-working, but
he was, perhaps, the luckiest. Chosen at
random to represent his school on this trip,
he could hardly believe he was really here.

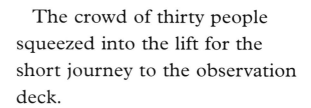

The crowd of thirty people squeezed into the lift for the short journey to the observation deck.

"Today we know that a comet is made up of a hard nucleus made of rock or ice. As the comet approaches the sun, some of this material burns off, creating the comet's tail," said the guide. "That's why the tail always points away from the sun."

When the doors opened there was an audible gasp from the crowd.

They had seen pictures of the observation deck, and watched the news reports. None of that had prepared them for the reality.

The huge dome seemed to open out on to space itself. The stars looked so near you could touch them.

Hanging there, silent in the perfect blackness of space, was the comet – a glittering silver firework with its tail spreading across a quarter of the sky.

Edward pushed his way forward to the front of the crowd.

The boy gazed up at the beautiful silver visitor and somehow found it hard to look away.

Timeline

240BC First identifiable sighting in Chinese records of Halley's Comet. It has been seen and recorded at every return since.

12BC Roman writings show the first record of Halley's Comet in European texts.

AD451 Halley's Comet is seen over Europe as the Romans defeat Attila the Hun.

AD837 Closest ever approach to Earth – 5,000,000 kilometres.

1066 Halley's Comet is seen before the Norman invasion of England. It appears on the Bayeux Tapestry.

1656 Edmund Halley is born.

1682 Edmund Halley observes the comet which will later be named after him.

1696 Halley calculates the orbits of many comets. He realises that the comets seen in the years 1531, 1607 and 1682 must actually be the same one. It is

the same comet that returns roughly every 76 years. Halley predicts its return but knows that he would have to live to be 102 years old to see the comet again.

1742   Edmund Halley dies aged 85.

1758   The returning comet is sighted on Christmas Day, proving Halley and his ideas correct.

1910   Halley's Comet is photographed for the first time.

1986   The most recent return of Halley's Comet. Space probes sent back the first close-up photographs of the comet.

2061   The next predicted return of Halley's Comet.

Glossary

astronomer   a scientist who studies the movement of the stars and planets

calculate   to work out a difficult maths problem

comet   an object made of rock and dust which orbits around the sun. The word 'comet' comes from the Greek word 'Kometes' meaning 'hairy star'.

gravity   the force which pulls one object towards another. The Earth's gravity is what pulls things 'down' towards the ground

lens   a specially shaped piece of glass used in telescopes and spectacles

nucleus   the centre of something

observation   when you see something and write it down

orbit   the scientific word for a planet or comet's curved path around a sun

plague   a deadly disease which can kill many people

predict   to describe the future before it happens

solar system   a star and the planets and comets which travel round it

Sun   the yellow star at the centre of our solar system which gives out heat and light

telescope   an instrument that makes objects in the distance look bigger